A ROYAL ADVENTURE

The Chronicles of Chloe

Shauna Forde

Ordinary Matters Publishing

Ordinary Matters Publishing
www.ordinarymatterspublishing.com

Publisher's Note: This is a work of fiction. Names, characters, places, and incidents are a product of the author's imagination. Locales and public names are sometimes used for atmospheric purposes. Any resemblance to actual people, living or dead, or to businesses, companies, events, institutions, or locales is completely coincidental.

Book Layout © 2014 BookDesignTemplates.com

A Royal Adventure/ Shauna Forde. -- 1st ed.
ISBN-13: 978-1941303177
ISBN-10: 194130317X

To all those who love fairytales
and still dream of happily ever after.

*I think every young girl at some point in her early life
wonders what it's like to be a princess. They like the idea
of dressing up and the fun of it....*

—JULIE ANDREWS

A NOTE TO MY READERS

If you love a fun short read, then you'll love *A ROYAL ADVENTURE*. You can enjoy this story over a lunch break, a train or bus ride, or just sitting in your favorite comfy chair.

I hope you enjoy the story and meeting Chloe, the main character, as much as I had coming up with her and her story.

Love Chloe? Visit my Facebook page and let me know. I love to hear from my readers.

Visit www.ShaunaForde.com for news, info on my new book releases, and especially for a free copy of my upcoming book ISLAND BILLION-AIRE.

Now, it's time to read. Have fun!

Shauna Forde
www.ShaunaForde.com

CONTENTS

A ROYAL ADVENTURE

THE INVITATION

C hloe sat in front of the computer staring at her hands. What was wrong with them? Why wouldn't the words come the way they had when she was younger? In seventh grade she wrote the best story ever told by anyone her age. In fact, she had won the top honor in her school and even got mentioned by the local writer's club. But as the years had passed and she HAD to write for income, that creative spark that burned inside her had become harder and harder to ignite.

Buster licked Chloe's feet as she sat at the desk. "Stop," she giggled, slowly pulling the little Yorkie onto her lap. She stroked the soft silky hair and let Buster happily lick her face. "I know, I know," she said, wiping the dog slobber off her cheeks. "You love me, don't you?" Chloe thought about her current situation. Even though she wasn't making a

2 · SHAUNA FORDE

penny from writing, she was earning a few bucks watching Buster while her neighbor was away on a two week cruise to Alaska. "And I love you too," she said, smiling down at the dog that brought cute to a whole new level.

Chloe jumped when she heard her phone start singing. She changed her ringtone more often than she changed her hairstyle... and that was a lot! She looked down at the number and even though she didn't recognize it, she answered. "Hello?"

"Hello, is this Miss Chloe Heffenpepper?" the voice asked in a tight British accent.

"Yes, this is Chloe," she answered, curiously.

"Miss Chloe Heffenpepper of 345 Ballister Lane?"

Chloe thought before answering, uneasy about giving out her address. What the heck, she thought. She was an out of work writer with nothing better to do than dog-sit on a Saturday night.

"Yes... who is this?"

"Miss Heffenpepper, this is Reginald Stebens. The honor of your presence has been requested at the Admiral's Ball to be held this Saturday forthcoming at 7 o'clock. Details will be forwarded to you posthaste."

"Wha..." Chloe stopped, wondering what this person had just said and what kind of joke it was. Before she could answer, Buster jumped from her lap and ran to the door barking furiously. Chloe snapped her attention back to her cell phone and was about to speak when she noticed that Mr. Reginald Stebens had hung up on her. Too flustered to be angry, she got up from the chair and went to see what Buster was fixated on.

She followed Buster's barking to the front door and when she looked through the side window to see who was there, she noticed a large letter leaning against the door. Chloe peeked around the front porch to see who might have left it, but no one was there. She glanced behind her, wondering if someone was spying on her and playing a really good prank. Satisfied that they weren't, she opened the door and grabbed the letter.

She sat down on the chair in the hall, ripped the envelope open and hoped that it was an acceptance letter from a book publishing company. She held her breath and read. "Dear Miss Chloe Heffenpepper,

His Royal Admiral Simon Peters requests your presence at a ball in his honor Saturday, March 24th at Castle de la Mer."

Chloe read the rest of the invitation and tried to absorb the details of this wildly, weird thing. Well, it definitely wasn't an acceptance letter. An invitation, from a Royal Admiral, for her? As if that wasn't bizarre enough, the outside of the invitation was addressed to Her Royal Highness, Miss Chloe Heffenpepper. Royal Highness? Chloe had been called a lot of things in her life, especially with a last name like Heffenpepper. But never, ever had anyone called her Royal Highness.

She took the invitation and the envelope and tromped back to the computer with Buster on her heels. Her fingers started to work again and Chloe began clicking away on the keys. There was plenty of information about Admiral Simon Peterson. Chloe discovered that not only was the Admiral the son of a Canadian Royal dignitary, he was also actually of royal lineage. Chloe dug a little further and discovered that he was also very wealthy. To top it all off, he was young and extremely handsome.

Chloe sat back and called Buster back onto her lap. She stroked his hair with one hand while the other clicked the mouse, scanning page after page on Simon Peterson. She wondered if the invitation was a mistake. But then she recalled the voice on the phone reciting her address. And, she ran her fingers over the expensive parchment the invitation was printed on; it was clearly addressed to her. She couldn't imagine that there were too many Chloe Heffenpeppers around. Nope, she thought.

Heffenpepper. The name had stuck with her like a bad reputation. The irony was that the name wasn't probably her legal name anyhow. Chloe had been brought up by a single mother who had died when Chloe was only nine. She never knew her father and according to her one living relative, her Aunt Genie, no one knew who he was. Genie had taken her in after her mother had passed, and although Genie was quite eccentric, she was the only family Chloe had, and she loved her.

After graduating in the middle of her class, Chloe went off to college. It wasn't until then that she realized just how lonely she felt not having any other family. She had longed for a father, brothers, sisters and cousins. Chloe had always felt a pinch of sadness when friends would talk of large family gatherings over the holidays. Genie had a ton of friends, and so did Chloe. But it wasn't the same as family.

Chloe had recently returned home with a degree in English Literature. She had hoped to secure a job right away and not have to burden Genie by moving back in. But Genie was glad to have her.

"No, no dear. Don't be silly. This is your home, and you are always welcome," said Genie, making up a separate office area for Chloe to pursue her career. "Besides, having the pressure of an apartment and bills will stifle those creative juices. Here," Genie said, extending her arm toward the nook in the corner of the living room, "you can write undisturbed and let your creativity flow!"

Chloe had reluctantly accepted Genie's offer. After all, she couldn't deny the wisdom behind it. So with her degree freshly mounted on the wall above the computer, Chloe set out to win the next Pulitzer Prize. But even with the proper Feng Shui balance of plants, natural light, and running water, all Chloe had managed to land were some short story gigs and opportunities to write on free share sites. Aunt Genie had never once asked her for a penny. But at twenty-two years old and four months after graduating, Chloe was seriously questioning her writing abilities.

She knew she was a good writer, but doubt had begun to creep in. Some of her advisors had suggested that perhaps she consider pursuing a teaching certificate or maybe continue on for her master's degree. Chloe had politely declined, sure she would be signing books at sold out appearances by now. But as she looked at her name on the invitation in front of her, she realized it might be the only time she would see her name in print.

"Ugh," she said, exasperated at the thought of having to go back to school. Buster licked her arm and Chloe looked down at the cute dog. "Ugh," she said again. Despite not having to pay any rent or bills of any kind, Chloe still tried to contribute. In order to help Aunt Genie out and to support herself to some degree, Chloe had resorted to picking up freelance virtual secretarial work, and as a favor to her neighbors, had agreed to dog-sit Buster for a few weeks while they cruised around Alaska. Why anyone who lived in Minnesota would want to go to Alaska was beyond her.

"But I'd do it again in a heartbeat," Chloe said as she kissed Buster.

THE DRESS

"**W**ell, what do you think?" Chloe asked Tracy as she nibbled on her Caesar salad. "A mistake? A total mix-up?"

Tracy read and re-read the invitation as she sipped on her Bloody Mary. "I don't know Chloe. It doesn't look like a mistake. I mean they spelled your name right and everything. How often does that happen?"

Chloe just rolled her eyes. "You're right, I know. But why would they invite me?"

Tracy took a long sip on her cocktail. She flipped the invitation over and over in her perfectly mani-cured fingers. Chloe and Tracy had been friends since elementary school. Tracy was the youngest of six children and had a huge extended Italian fami-ly. They got together every Sunday for sauce – which was really a giant spaghetti dinner and lots of gossip. Tracy had spent many Sundays there and always mourned a little when she returned home to the quiet of her life with Aunt Genie.

But despite their differences, Tracy and Chloe had remained best of friends through the years. Tracy had also just graduated but unlike Chloe, she had been hired right from school by the firm she interned for in her final year of earning her market-ing degree.

Tracy took another long sip and then stopped. Her mouth flew open, and the straw fell out. "Wait a minute! Your name is online, right? I mean you've written a bunch of stuff, even interviews, and stuff online, right?"

Chloe put her fork down and thought for minute. "Yeah," she said, unsure where Tracy was going with this.

"I bet they came across your name online and mistook you for a reputable reporter," Tracy said, smiling over her straw.

"Thanks a lot," said Chloe sarcastically. But as she thought about it, Tracy was probably right. It was the only explanation that made any sense.

After lunch, Chloe scanned the internet for the interviews she had published online. There was only a handful, and, she had to admit, they weren't very good. But still, that had to be why she was being invited. She looked up other royal affairs and found that even though the paparazzi were not attendees, they still dressed formally. This meant that she too would have to wear a formal gown.

Just the thought of trying on gowns made Chloe's stomach turn. She had always been skinny, even as a very little girl. And she wasn't skinny in the slim, athletic sort of way. Chloe had been the nerdy skinny. When she was in middle school she had short curly blond hair, glasses, and braces. By the time she got to high school, Chloe started to disappear in Tracy's shadow. Tracy had gorgeous long black hair and curves in all the right places. She never acted like all eyes were on her, but they were. Eventually, Chloe had agreed to let Tracy give her a makeover. And as the years went by, her hair grew, the braces came off, and the contacts went in. But the thin frame stayed with her. And now, Chloe had one day to come up with a gown that made her look royal.

"C'mon, you'll look amazing," said Tracy as she coaxed Chloe into the next shop. "Trust me."

"I do trust you, it's just that no matter how beautiful the dress, I'll still have this." Chloe pointed down to her legs. They were skinny and pale and tapered sharply to her ankles. Chicken legs, that's what Aunt Genie had always called them. Not just because of how scrawny they were. But also because of the birthmark on her ankle. It was a cluster of freckles that was actually shaped like a chicken leg.

"Don't worry about that. With this dress," Tracy said, pointing to the emerald green gown in the mirror, "nobody is going to be looking at your feet."

Tracy was right. The dress was made of the smoothest satin Chloe had ever felt. The lace bodice was tight and flattering, showing just enough of Chloe's minimal cleavage to make it look like more than it was. The waist was adorned with beading that disappeared into the full length skirt. Slim straps held the bodice delicately against Chloe's ivory skin. The green was almost exactly the same color as the green of her eyes. And when she stood in front of the mirror and looked at herself, she knew Tracy was right. She looked amazing. Nobody would even notice her birthmark.

After hours of shopping, Chloe returned home to the smell of baking cookies.

"I love it," said Aunt Genie. "Now, you must be exhausted. What do you say we spend the evening watching movies and eating junk food? That way you'll be sure and fill that dress out all the way!"

Tracy kissed Genie on the cheek, glad that even though she was the only family she had, she had her. "Okay, let me just hang this up and I'll be right back."

The two women spent the rest of the night baking, laughing, and reminiscing about Chloe's mother. "You look so much like her, you know," Genie said. Chloe knew her aunt missed her sister Jasmine terribly. Genie often said that the day Jasmine had died had been the worst, but also one of the best because it was the day she took custody of Chloe.

"I know," Chloe said, thinking of all the pictures she had seen of her mother. She did look like her. She had the same blond hair, the same green eyes, and the same slight frame. "Except..."

"For the chicken leg!" the two women said at the same time in a burst of laughter. After indulging in cookies and watching a sappy movie, the two women fell fast asleep on the sofa.

Chloe woke up to the sound of Buster coughing. She jumped off the sofa and ran across the room to him and saw he was choking on something. Aunt Genie woke up from the commotion and the two women pry open his mouth and pull out a long, wet, piece of cloth.

"What the…" Chloe said, looking at the sopping wet cloth. Genie pulled the rest of it out and held it up. Their eyes met, and instantly they both realized what it was.

"The dress!" The women shouted and ran to the bedroom. The white garment bag was still zipped at the top, but the bottom was ripped open. On the floor, underneath the frayed garment bag, lay the shredded green dress and a pile of cookie crumbs.

"Buster!" Chloe yelled in a panic. She looked at Aunt Genie. "The ball is two days away! I'll never have enough time to find another dress."

"Let's see if we can find a dress shop to fix it up," Genie said, gathering the pieces off the floor.

Genie took the dress and disappeared out of the room as Chloe ran to the computer. She doubted she could find anybody to fix the mess Buster made, let alone fix it in a day. She opened the internet to find her email flooded with new rejection letters. Tears stung the corner of her eyes as she tried to keep it together. She knew it wasn't Buster's fault; he was just a silly dog. And she didn't want Genie to see her lose it. She thought about the ball again and resolved to think positively. Maybe,

Chloe thought, just maybe this will be my big break.

Chloe never set out to be a reporter. But if that's what it took her to get noticed, she would do it. Having her name in print and being seen as a serious writer was all she wanted. If she had to start as a reporter, she could work up from there. Besides, many reporters go on to have great careers and even publish books.

She spent hours searching shop after shop, calling one after the other until she finally found one that would do the work. "Oh, thank you," Chloe said, feeling the worry dissipate. "Just one more thing," she said, pausing. "How much will this cost?"

Chloe held her breath and let it out in a rush when she heard the response on the other end of the phone. "Three hundred and fifty for same day," the lady at the shop said. "That's if we can find fabric that will match."

"Thank you," said Chloe as she hung the phone up, feeling the claws of defeat again. She looked at her computer, trying not to count the rejection emails, but knowing they outnumbered the job offers exponentially. She thought maybe she should just give up. Why even bother to be a writer? Why even bother to be a reporter? Why even bother to look good when she was just a plain Jane, unemployed college graduate with chicken legs.

Buster came bouncing into the room to brighten her spirits. But this time, Chloe was anything but happy to see him. She brushed him aside and sat on the edge of the bed, picking off the green strands of dress that clung to her pants. But Buster wouldn't leave her alone.

"What? What do you want now?" Chloe asked impatiently. Buster kept pulling at her and barking until she couldn't ignore him. "Okay, I'll come," she said as she followed him out into the living room. She stopped when she saw Aunt Genie. She was holding a green dress that looked similar to the one Chloe had bought. But it was different. In place of the ripped skirt was a collection of multicolored fabric strips that hung vertically from the waistline. Each strip was finished with the same green lace of the bodice. Chloe looked at the dress, at Aunt Genie, and then at the dress again. Her aunt, her loving aunt, had taken the destroyed remnants of the dress and turned it into a work of beauty, a dress fit for a queen.

"Thank you," Chloe said as she ran and threw her arms around Genie. "I love it – and I love you!" She planted a wet kiss on her aunt's cheek, grabbed the dress, and headed back to her room, closing the door behind her ensuring Buster was on the other side.

With the dress problem solved, Chloe focused on learning more about the family she would be interviewing so she would be prepared for her big break. She went back online and discovered that Simon Peterson's father was the Admiral Chief Emory Francis Peterson of the Royal Canadian Fleet. He was a direct descendent of the royal family of England by marriage. But his wife had died years ago, when his son, Simon Peterson, was only eleven.

"Hmmm," Chloe said out loud to herself. "His mother died when he was young, too." Chloe thought that was very interesting.

She continued researching and discovered that the Admiral's ball was an annual event and that this year the ball was honoring Simon Peterson and his advancement to the position of Vice Admiral in the Royal Fleet. Chloe didn't know what any of that meant, but knew it sounded important. She continued to look for any connections she might have to this event or the family, again wondering how they found her. She was just a small town girl from Minnesota. This was a big, royal Canadian family. She couldn't even begin to see how their paths would have ever crossed.

After searching for hours, Chloe figured she wouldn't find anything else. She grabbed the invitation and saw that it told her to expect a car to pick her up at 5:00 for the event. A car, thought Chloe? Wow! If they treated reporters like this, she couldn't imagine how they treated the royalty!

Chloe spent the rest of the night figuring out how to approach the task ahead of her. Should she bring her recorder? Her iPod? Her tablet? She certainly didn't want to lug her laptop with her. She had a nice small evening bag that would hold her iPod or recorder nicely. But was she allowed to record? She had never been to such a formal event before and didn't want to break protocol. But she also didn't want the royal family to see her inexperience. After all, this just might be her big break.

And then there was Buster. She had to make sure she was home on time because even though Tracy had agreed to come watch him for a few hours, she didn't want to put her out. Aunt Genie would have done it, but she had her weekly Bikram meditation class. Chloe never understood why Aunt Genie kept going to those classes. She was flexible and so relaxed and at peace, why did she need to keep going to those things? Genie would tell her it was because she kept going that she was so relaxed and at peace. She also hinted to Chloe many times that perhaps she should try the class and maybe it would help remove her writer's block. But Chloe was pretty certain that if she had to sit in the lotus position for very long, her little chicken legs just might snap.

THE ADMIRAL'S BALL

The day of the ball was a perfect September day. The air was crisp and the sun was bright. Tracy came over in the afternoon to help Chloe get ready for the big event.

"You look beautiful," said Genie, giving her niece a kiss on the cheek. "I'll see you tonight. I can't wait to hear all about it…" and she was off to meditation.

"She's right," said Tracy, looking at her best friend. "You do look beautiful. I didn't think it was possible to make the dress any prettier than it was, but you guys did it."

"Actually," Chloe said, looking down at the dog. "Buster did it!"

The two girls laughed and put the finishing touches on Chloe's look just as the doorbell rang. They turned and looked at each other, realizing this was it – Chloe's big moment. Chloe grabbed her purse and slipped on her shoes. Tracy grabbed Buster and the two girls ran to the door, swung it open, and froze. A man in a chauffer's suit, complete with a hat and all, stood ramrod straight in front of them with both gloved hands clasped behind his back.

The girls looked at him, then at each other and giggled. Then they looked past the driver. At the end of the little brick walkway, parked in front of the house, was a shining white stretch limousine.

"Miss Heffenpepper, I'm Kent, and I'll be your driver for the evening." Kent held out one gloved hand. When Chloe stuck hers out for a handshake, Kent blinked twice and then gently grabbed Chloe's hand, held it up in his and kissed it.

"Wow," said Tracy. "They really do treat the help well, don't they?" she said, holding an excited Buster. "Have a great time, love you." She planted a big kiss on Chloe's cheek and then stepped back inside the doorway, letting Chloe and Kent make their way to the awaiting car.

Kent opened the back door and helped Chloe inside. She slid onto the luxurious leather seat and was immediately enveloped with the scent of filthy rich. "Wow," she said in a whisper. It took Kent almost a full minute to make his way all the way back up to the driver's seat.

"I hope you are finding everything to your liking?" Kent asked, never taking his eyes off the road as they pulled out into traffic.

"To my liking? Um," Chloe didn't know what to say. "Um, yeah, very much!" Who was she kidding? This guy was a working stiff just like her. She figured she could get some information out of him on the ride.

"So, how long of a ride is it?" Chloe asked Kent, looking at his expressionless face in the very distant rear view.

"Just a little while, less than twenty minutes."

"Huh, and how many other reporters will be there?" Chloe asked as she slid up to the front of the sofa, trying to get closer to Kent.

"I don't know, madam," Kent said stiffly.

"And why me, do you know why I'm going?" Chloe figured she better get right to it. Kent wasn't opening up very easily, and she only had twenty minutes.

"I'm sorry madam, I'm not privileged to that information."

After several more attempts at getting information, Chloe realized Kent wasn't going to budge. They pulled off the main road and meandered down a long, beautifully landscaped, paved road that led to the estate. As they rounded a thick of hedges, the Castle de la Mer loomed up in front of them in all its regal glory. One of Minnesota's thousand lakes glistened in the background, behind the lush green back lawn of the estate.

"Wow," Chloe said in a hushed voice. She had looked the castle up online and knew a little about its history. But to see it in person, in real life, was truly impressive.

Kent pulled into the circular driveway and stopped at the bottom of the castle steps. He walked around and opened Chloe's door and escorted her out of the limousine as she stepped out onto the flagstone walkway. She looked up and caught her breath as she took in the beauty around her.

"Madam," a voice said. Chloe turned to see the handsome young man from the internet standing next to her with a gloved hand out. Admiral Simon Peterson was even more delicious looking in real life.

"May I have the honor of escorting you?" he said, his bright blue eyes glistening like the medals on his uniform.

"Um, yes, of course," Chloe said, caught off guard. Why would the Admiral want to take a lowly reporter into the ball? Chloe wondered if it was protocol for the person being honored to escort the ladies down the red carpet. Perhaps only she was being escorted. Oh, thought Chloe. Maybe I'll get an exclusive.

They ascended the steps together and when Chloe got to the top, she let go of the Admiral's hand and pulled her little notepad out of her purse in full view of all the on-lookers. She felt so important, like she was a top-notch reporter with all eyes on her. In fact, she quickly noticed she was the only reporter there. Wow, she thought, it WAS an exclusive! These Peterson people must think she was really good.

The Admiral was immediately flanked by several young, attractive women. Chloe cleared her throat and disappeared into the castle, getting lost in the crowd of party goers. Well, it was fun while it lasted, as she thought of the handsome escort. She began looking around, taking in all the sights and smells. People of every age and high station filled the room with laughter and chatter. White-clothed butlers walked through the crowd with silver trays of finger foods and shimmering crystal flutes of champagne.

Chloe recognized some of the revelers from their pictures in the society pages and online magazines. There were celebrities, heads of state, politicians and even a few musicians. She approached each of them with courage, knowing that it was now or never and she had to go for it. The celebrities and musicians humored her with a few lines for her interview. But the politicians, especially the Canadian ones, were less than accommodating. Every time Chloe approached them to get a sound bite they would bow awkwardly and move away as if they were clearing room for her. She just couldn't get close enough to get anyone to give her an interview.

"Are you enjoying yourself?" Simon asked, walking up behind Chloe.

"Oh," she replied, startled. "Oh, yes, I'm enjoying this very much. Thank you for the invitation. I mean, I know you don't know me, and this is a special day and all...." Chloe stammered. She didn't usually get nervous, but those piercing blue eyes made focus nearly impossible.

"Yes, it is a special day," said Simon, smiling with his whole face.

"So," Chloe went on, trying to stay professional. "When do we do it?"

Simon looked at her and laughed. "Do it? Well, you really are straightforward, aren't you?"

"Well," Chloe said, not sure what he expected. "I want to make sure I have you alone for at least a few minutes, so we can do this with no distractions. But I can wait until after the ceremony."

She grabbed a chocolate-covered strawberry off a passing silver platter and plucked it into her mouth. "It doesn't matter. I'm easy."

Simon laughed again and opened his mouth to speak just as a drop-dead gorgeous red-head slid her arm in his.

"Simon," she purred. "I've been looking everywhere for you. Are you trying to avoid me?" Her thick lashes and hazel eyes batted above her pouty lips.

Chloe noticed Simon roll his eyes as he turned toward the bombshell. "Madeline," Simon said as he patted her hand and gently removed it from his arm.

"I'm so sorry to interrupt," Madeline continued, obviously not sorry to interrupt. "But I really wanted to talk to you," she said, as she tried in vain to encircle his arm again.

"Madeline," Simon interrupted her, waving his arm out to Chloe. "Have you met?" He looked back and forth between the two.

Chloe looked up at the tall, statuesque woman and stuck out her hand. "Hi," she said as she finished chewing the strawberry. "I'm Chloe."

Madeline seemed wholly disinterested. In fact, Chloe didn't think she even heard her. But then Simon spoke.

"This is Chloe," he said, looking sternly at Madeline. "Chloe Heff-en-pepp-er." Simon drew out Chloe's last name for emphasis, or Chloe thought, maybe he just didn't know if he was saying it right.

Either way, as soon as Madeline heard the name, she dropped Simon's hand and a flush of embarrassment rose in her cheeks. "I'm so sorry, please forgive me," she said, bowing her head and curtseying. She bobbed up and down and then stepped backwards into the crowd, not even lifting her head to make eye contact with Chloe.

"That was weird," Chloe said.

Simon just shook his head and smiled. "You don't have any idea what tonight's all about, do you?"

"Well, I'm trying to figure that out. But people here have been less than cooperative," Chloe said, exasperated.

Simon walked over and stood next to her. "Okay," he said, surveying the crowd with her. "There," he said, pointing to a woman in a fur stole. "Do you see that woman?"

Chloe nodded and put her pen to pad, ready to write. Simon went on. "That's Lady Winifred, of the Chamberlain family. And that bloke," Simon pointed to a man with a handlebar mustache and a top hat. "He's the Duke of Emerald House."

Chloe took notes on everything Simon said and tried hard not to think about how intoxicating he smelled. She kept her eyes focused on the crowd and her notes rather than Simon. If he wanted to give her personal information, he would. If not, so be it. She didn't really care how the interview went. He was in charge, and she was willing to do it his way.

"And that," Simon pointed to a tall, dark haired, middle aged man, adorned with regal colors and medals. "That is Prince Philip Oliver Doussard."

"Oh," Chloe said in awe, not having a clue who that was. "Is he important?"

Simon laughed out loud. "Yes, yes, he's very important. In fact, he's the reason –"

"Ladies and Gentlemen," the voice echoed in the castle walls. "Ladies and Gentlemen, please find your seats in Montclair Hall as the ceremony is about to begin.

"He's the reason for what?" Chloe asked Simon. But he had been beckoned away by another middle-aged man in full military regalia. Chloe shrugged and followed the crowd through the large doors leading into Montclair Hall. Seats were lined up in rows all the way to the ornately decorated stage. Musicians played violins and harps on either side and the center of the stage was adorned with a red carpet staircase leading up to a solid oak podium.

Chloe surveyed the room and the crowd. She didn't see any designated press seats and was forced to sit in the middle of the room. The ceremony began with trumpeters announcing the arrival of the distinguished guests. After several stuffy dignitaries were announced, the trumpeters again blew.

Chloe looked around for Simon but couldn't see him. She assumed he was just offstage, waiting to be announced. Even though Chloe had never attended one of these events before, she had seen movies. The horn blowers dropped their horns, and the lead trumpeter turned to face the audience.

"His royalty, the Admiral Chief Emory Francis Peterson of the Royal Canadian Fleet," announced the trumpeter without blinking an eye. The only thing that moved was the chinstrap of his hat and his mouth. Chloe wondered how he could stand so still while yelling so loudly.

She watched as the Admiral Chief emerged from behind the velvet curtain and made his way to the left of the podium. All of the other people on stage stood while clapping his arrival. The audience stood and sat with the announcement of each guest. Chloe remained standing just a hair longer than everyone else to see if she could catch a glimpse of that handsome Simon again. And then the trumpets blew again.

"Really?" Chloe said out loud, earning her a nasty look from an old man next to her. She smiled shyly as if to say, "sorry." Then she turned back toward the stage just as the trumpeter announced Simon. Everyone was on their feet again, cheering the arrival of the dashing young Admiral. Simon walked out looking as handsome as ever, but this time with his military sword hanging from his belt. The sleek metal flashed brilliantly underneath the crystal chandeliers, and Chloe clapped furiously.

Simon made his way to the right of the podium and stood alone. Now that everyone was in attendance, Chloe assumed they would get on with the celebration. But then another guest was announced.

The trumpeters blew and the lead trumpeter announced, "His Highness Prince Philip Oliver Doussard." With this the entire room erupted. Everyone on the stage, including Simon and his parents, turned to welcome the Prince to the stage. Chloe watched as the tall, regal looking gentleman made his way through the guests and over to Simon's father, shaking hands and kissing cheeks.

He must really be some big deal, thought Chloe. The Prince walked around the back of the podium and saluted Simon and then let him rest at ease before turning toward the guests.

"Distinguished guests, friends and family," began the Prince. "It is my honor to welcome you to the 130th Annual Admiral's Ball." The crowd cheered. Chloe didn't realize it was the 130th ball.

This truly was an historic event. She made a quick note figuring she better mention that in her write-up.

"Tonight we are here to commemorate the advancement of Captain Simon Peterson to the rank of Vice Admiral," said the Prince, to another round of raucous applause. He went on for several minutes, talking about Simon's accomplishments as Simon sat quietly and humbly took it all in. Chloe knew she had to get up front if she wanted to get a chance to pepper him with questions before other people got the scoop on her. Even though there wasn't a press section, she knew this event was being covered by other reporters. And she was not about to let this chance get away from her.

Finally, the talking was done and another man in full-dress uniform came out to the stage and presented a wooden box to the Prince. He opened it and called Simon's father to accompany him to Simon. They flanked Simon as he stood and each saluted him before taking the shiny medal of rank out of the box. With his father at his side, Simon stood at attention while the Prince pinned the medal to his uniform lapel. A hush fell over the crowd and when he was done, Prince Philip took a step back, stood at attention and saluted the new Vice Admiral. When the salute was dismissed, Prince Philip presented Simon to the guests.

"May I present to you, his royalty, Vice Admiral Simon Peterson of the Royal Canadian Fleet!" The room broke out in loud cheers and applause. Chloe seized the opportunity and ran up to the stage just as Simon moved up to the podium.

Before he could say a word, Chloe begins peppering him with questions. "Vice Admiral, how do you feel being advanced at such a young age? Do you feel you deserve the rank? Do you believe that you will make a good Vice Admiral? What are your future career aspirations?"

She stood perfectly still in her colorful evening gown with pen and notebook in hand. It wasn't until she saw Simon put his hand up that Chloe realized the room had fallen silent. She stopped and stared in horror as she realized that no one else in the room was asking questions. Simon lowered his hand, and Chloe wished she could disappear. But she couldn't; she was standing at the front of the room, in a brilliantly colored evening gown, holding a pen and notebook with two hundred pairs of eyes on her.

The guests started chattering in a low murmur and Simon again put up his hand. The Admiral Chief and the Prince stood silent, staring down at Chloe, and she felt the embarrassment rise up in her cheeks.

"Please," said Simon to quiet the crowd. "Please, silence, please," he said sternly but kindly. When the crowd quieted, Simon walked around the front of the podium and down the red carpeted steps toward Chloe.

She stood frozen with fear. Why was he doing this? Was he trying to embarrass her? She knew she had screwed up, but this was just mean. She wanted to run out of there with every fiber in her being but she was paralyzed. Simon reached the bottom of the steps and stood in front of her – and bowed and extended his hand to her.

Chloe was too confused to refuse. She set her hand in his gloved one and he turned and escorted her up the steps and onto the stage. The Prince walked over to her, looked her up and down, and then looked at her feet. After a quick glance, he looked back up at her and smiled as one tear rolled down his cheek. He took her other hand in his and together he and Simon turned to face the crowd with Chloe in the middle.

"May I present to you," said Prince Philip, "Her Royal Highness, Princess Chloe Heffenpepper Doussard." Chloe felt the world close in on her. She heard the words, but didn't believe them. Chloe stood frozen as the crowd applauded. A second later, all the pieces fell into place, and she realized what had just happened. Then she fainted.

Chloe woke up to Simon, his father, Prince Philip, and several other attendants surrounding her and fanning her. She was in a private room in the castle, and everyone told her what had happened as her head began to clear.

"Chloe," said Philip as he held her hand in his.

"I never knew, I never knew I had a daughter, I didn't know about you," he said through his tears. He went on to tell Chloe that he had met Jasmine one summer while she was visiting Canada. The two fell in love. But the Prince never revealed his true identity to her. Instead, he claimed to be an ensign in the Navy. He feared women only liked him for his money. But Jasmine was different and he knew it. He had planned on revealing his true identity the day before he was to be deployed. But by then, Jasmine had returned back to Minnesota. With only their first names, neither had any way of tracking the other down.

"It wasn't until just last year that someone came across a piece written by you with a picture on your bio," said the Prince. Chloe watched as he spoke. She could sense the love he had for her and she felt her own heart fill up in places that had been empty for so long.

"You see," said Philip. "You look just so much like her; you look just like her," he said kissing her hand. "But I had to be sure. So I had someone follow you and take pictures. You had the same hair, the same eyes, the same build. And," Philip looked around nervously, "you had the Doussard family birthmark."

The chicken leg, thought Chloe. Philip lifted up his pants leg and revealed the same birthmark on his ankle. Her eyes filled up with tears. "But still, I needed physical proof. So I had my men collect a discarded coffee cup and test it for DNA. That's how we knew where you lived and what you did for a living."

Philip looked at his daughter. "I hope you understand, I just had to be sure."

Chloe looked around as the rest of the room stared at the two of them. Mad? If he was some kooky stalker or ax murderer, yeah! But he was a prince! He was her father! How on earth could she be mad?!

Chloe just nodded as Philip continued. "Once it was confirmed, I wanted to meet you. But I was scared. I didn't want you to run away or not like me. I didn't know how to get you to come... so we devised this plan to have you as a guest at your own coming out party."

"I'm so sorry I tricked you," said Philip as he held her hand tightly. "And I'm so sorry for all the time we lost, and..." his voice trailed off. "For Jasmine. Chloe, I'm so sorry about Jasmine."

The room fell silent, and all eyes were on Chloe. She took a deep breath and looked around at the kind faces surrounding her. Simon sat by one side of her bed while Philip, Prince Philip, her father, sat on the other side. Simon's father stood behind Simon along with several other elegantly dressed people. Chloe scanned the room and let her eyes rest briefly on Simon. She smiled and then turned her attention to Philip.

"Prince Philip, I mean," Chloe hesitated, scared to utter the word she had waited her whole life to say. "I'm not sorry at all, father." Philip reached down and grabbed Chloe up into his arms. His strength was overpowering, and Chloe fought to catch her breath through her tears when he released her. After everyone calmed down, Chloe looked around and then again at her father.

"Just one more thing," she said as Philip smiled broadly.

"Yes, what is it dear? Anything you want?"

Chloe pointed over to Simon and then asked, "Are we related?"

Everyone laughed and then Philip smiled. "No dear, you are not related." Then he turned to Simon and smiled fondly. "At least, not yet."

Simon looked at Chloe and they both smiled, knowing their affection was mutual. The Prince and his daughter returned to the ball and enjoyed the rest of the evening. After another hour of introductions and visiting with aunts, uncles, aunts, half-brothers, half-sisters, nieces and nephews, Chloe could barely stand.

"You look tired," said Simon as he escorted her to the patio for some fresh air.

"Yes, I am," she said. "It's all just so overwhelming. I think I need to call it a night."

"Can I escort you back to the car, Princess Doussard?" Simon asked, holding his arm out for her. She still couldn't believe that was her name.

"You may," she giggled as she slid her arm in his and walked out to the flagstone driveway to her awaiting limousine.

Kent tipped his hat to Chloe and opened the door for her and then discreetly disappeared around the other side of the car, giving Chloe and Simon some privacy.

"So, will you be coming back soon?" Simon asked.

"Well," Chloe said, "I have already made arrangements to return this week and get to know everyone under less formal circumstances." She paused and then continued, looking up at Simon's bright eyes. "Besides, I've got a story to finish."

"Really?" Simon asked jokingly. "And how does it end?"

"The Princess lives happily ever after," Chloe said as she closed her eyes and let his full lips fall on hers. After all of the excitement of the day, Chloe wasn't sure she could survive anymore, but she was willing to take that chance for this kiss. And it was worth it.

HAPPILY EVER AFTER?

When Kent dropped her off at home, Chloe realized it was well past midnight and Buster and Aunt Genie were fast asleep. She found her way to her room and fell into a deep sleep right away. She awoke to Genie and Buster both panicking.

"Chloe, get up," yelled Genie, running around like a mad woman. Buster followed on Genie's heels, yapping up a storm.

Chloe figured she'd break the news slowly to Genie over a cup of coffee. But she didn't have that option. "What's the matter? What's wrong?" Chloe asked, worried something terrible had happened.

"Come quick," said Genie, running to the front door. Chloe threw on a robe and followed her aunt and the dog to the front door. Genie peeled the curtains back and pointed. Chloe blinked, not sure she was seeing what she was seeing.

"What's going on?" asked Genie. "They keep asking for you," Genie said, referring to the flock of reporters on the front lawn. "What happened at that ball last night?"

Chloe grabbed her aunt's hand, kissed her on the cheek, and then opened the door to the reporters. "Chloe, Chloe Doussard! How does it feel to be a royal princess and an heir to the Doussard family fortune?" The reporters peppered her with questions as Chloe just listened. Aunt Genie took it all in, realizing in short order what had transpired in her dear niece's life. She reached over and squeezed her hand, clearly happy for Chloe.

The questions continued and Chloe answered them as best she could. After several minutes she bid the reporters goodbye and turned to go back in the house.

"Chloe," came one final call from the crowd. "Chloe, have you thought about writing a book?"

Chloe stopped and turned back to the reporters. "I've thought about it my entire life," she said with a smile.

The two women went back inside and spent hours talking about the turn of events. When they were finished, Chloe went to her computer and checked her inbox absentmindedly. To her surprise, instead of the usual onslaught of rejection letters, Chloe's inbox was filled with offers from agents and publishers.

Buster jumped on Chloe's lap and licked her as she opened a new document and began typing. *"The Story of the Chicken Legged Princess"* – by Chloe Heffenpepper Doussard."

happily EVER after

BOOKS BY SHAUNA FORDE

THE BILLIONAIRE ROMANCE SERIES

One thing about the romance genre is that it constantly evolves. Today there are more new categories than ever before. The billionaire romance is a category I never thought I'd explore, but I was so wrong.

Why are so many readers attracted to the genre? Well, who wouldn't want to read about super-sexy men with boatloads of money and the women they attract?

But these new wealthy men have so much more than merely money. They have power and they aren't afraid to own it. Let's face it, they put the "A" in alpha male. Turn the page to see the new books coming this fall and spring.

THE BILLIONAIRE WEREWOLF CURSE

THE BILLIONAIRE GANGSTER

A BEAR'S SECRET

MORE BILLIONAIRE ROMANCE

ISLAND BILLIONAIRE

ISLAND BILLIONAIRE
SNEAK PEEK

Heaven De Lancelet stepped off the plane, setting foot on the island of Roatan and felt a wave of calmness penetrate every pore of her being. She felt home. She felt at peace. She felt connected. None of which made much sense given her high-pressure position in the book industry and the job at hand. At the very least, her friends and co-workers considered her driven. Still, the soft breeze caressed her body and made her relax and feel wanted. The very island air exerted a subtle pull upon her body as she moved toward the airport building.

Passengers pushed past her as Heaven tried to get her bearings. So much time had passed since her last visit to the island. The airport's facelift had been a success with more places to wait in sitting areas, coffee shops, and even a cafe or two. Already she knew much had changed but, she thought, so had she.

"Miss De Lancelet," a high voice cried out, and Heaven turned to see an older woman waving at her.

"Oh, Miss De Lancelet, I am so very happy to meet you at last. You must come with me now. I have a car and will be taking you to the lovely home where you will stay during your visit," the woman who carried a placard with Heaven's name said and guided Heaven past baggage. "You have bags, yes?"

"Yes---"

"Good, my husband will gather them. No need for you to worry, Miss. Come along."

Heaven's grasp on reality took effect and she came to a stop, nearly causing the woman to bump into a passerby. "Stop."

Wide-eyed and open-mouthed, the woman did as she was told.

"Who are you?" Heaven said, staring at the stranger who clearly was not an islander.

"Oh, I'm so sorry. I should have said. I'm just so excited--"

"I get that. Who are you?"

The woman extended her hand, "Why, I'm Mrs. Davenport, Mr. Burkhardt's assistant." Their two hands met and touched briefly.

That made sense. Would have been nice had the woman introduced herself. So the great Jared Burkhardt had this woman in his employ and had sent her to handle Heaven instead of showing up himself. Of course he did, she thought, wondering once again why she had agreed to make this trip. Clearly, the initial impact of the island was wearing off.

Then, all business, Mrs. Davenport started rattling off a few obvious housekeeping details she'd been told to deliver before reverting back to her escort duties and guided Heaven to the waiting car. Heaven settled into the back seat of the latest edition of the town car and checked her iPhone for texts and calls. At this point, she'd pretty much forgotten she was back on the island and was in full work mode. She knew she'd end up meeting with Jared all too soon. Truth told, she was quite happy to have been met by Mrs. Davenport. Facing Jared again was not something she had ever intended to do--ever.

FOR A FREE COPY, GO TO
http://www.ShaunaForde.com

ABOUT THE AUTHOR

Shauna Forde loves a good romance and lives in the great state of Texas with her pack of dogs and two cats. She invites you to explore the world of romance from romantic comedies to billionaire romances to stories of romance—even those with a tinge of mystery and odd happenings.

Join Shauna Forde (Author) on Facebook.

www.ShaunaForde.com

www.ingramcontent.com/pod-product-compliance
Lightning Source LLC
Chambersburg PA
CBHW050911120626

46552CB00004B/1514